Written by Benji Bennett.
benji@adamscloud.com

Illustrations by Roxanne Burchartz.
www.roxanneburchartz.com

Designed by Bold.
www.reallybold.com

This 2017 edition printed in Ireland by Watermans Printers.
www.watermansprinters.ie

ISBN 978-1-906818-06-7

Published by

An imprint of Adam's Printing Press Publishing.

Adam's Cloud is dedicated to spreading Adam's message of the importance of love, laughter and play within the family
and will make a donation from the proceeds of all books published under its imprint to children's charities.

Adam's Cloud
PO Box 11379, Blackrock, Co. Dublin, Ireland.
Email: info@adamscloud.com
Web: www.adamscloud.com
Tel: +353 1 2833620

2% of the proceeds from the sale of this book will go to

Anam Cara is a national voluntary organisation dedicated to supporting bereaved parents through a range of online and face to face support services.
Recognising the devastation families experience after the death of a child, Anam Cara provides a safe, comfortable place where parents can connect with other parents to
comfort and support each other. All Anam Cara services are available to families free of charge. For more information please visit www.anamcara.ie or email info@anamcara.ie

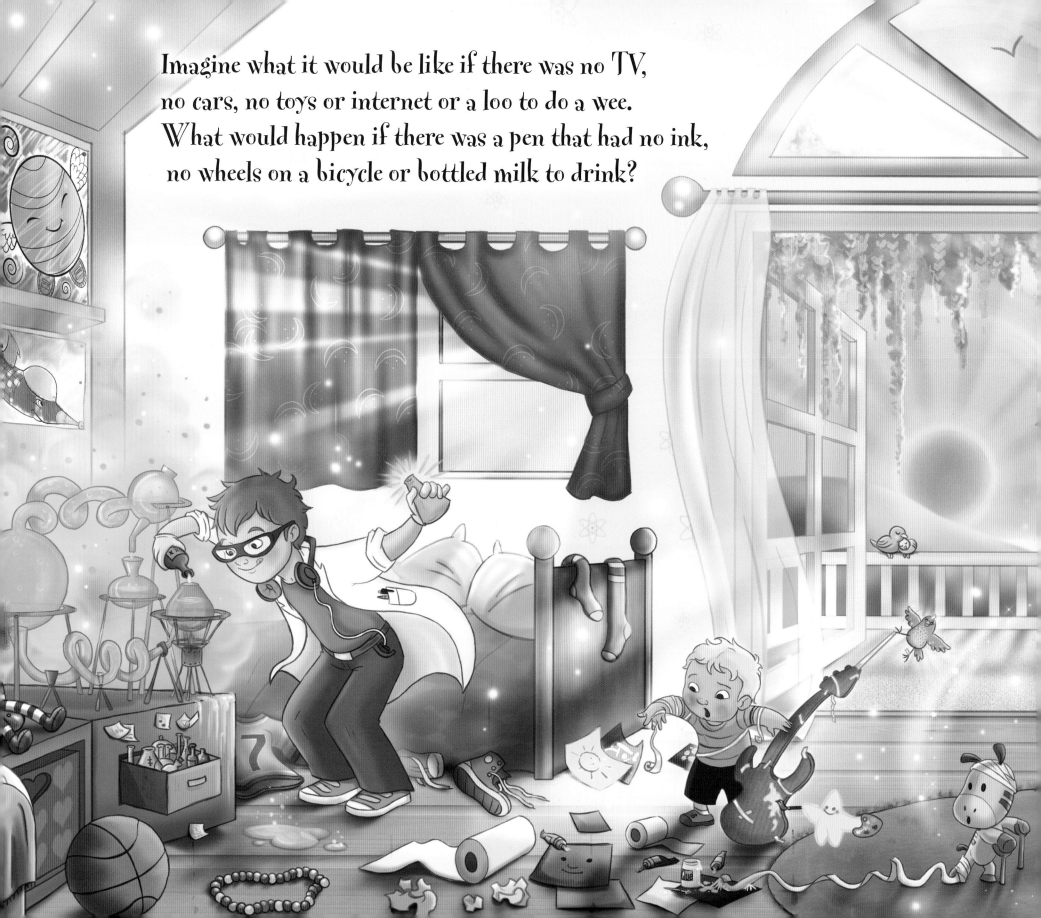

Imagine what it would be like if there was no TV,
no cars, no toys or internet or a loo to do a wee.
What would happen if there was a pen that had no ink,
no wheels on a bicycle or bottled milk to drink?

To Adam, our sweetheart,
with love, hugs and kisses from
Mum, Dad, Harry, Robbie and Molly.

Adam is an angel and lives on a cloud
and makes his Mummy and Daddy so proud.
With long golden hair you just could not miss,
he always has time for a hug and a kiss.
The message he sends from his cloud every day,
is to spend more time with each other and play.
The most important thing in life is this,
show your love for your family with a hug and a kiss.

Well! All the things we use and need each and every day
were invented by inventors to help us live and play.
"Inventors must be special people," said Adam with delight,
"Come on Fluff, let's fly and meet some before we sleep tonight."

"Weeeeee!" Off they flew upon Fluff's back on a new adventure to fly through space and back in time to find the best inventor.

Spinning round and round and upside down back in time to history bound hold on tight, what's this they found when Fluff landed on the ground.

"Oh my goodness," Adam said, "we're here, at the beginning
of history where the earth was young and one day started spinning.
"Welcome friends," a caveman said, "this is no dream, it's real
you're just in time to witness the invention of the wheel.

Bikes and trikes and motor cars, trucks and aeroplanes
would never work without the wheel thanks to my clever brains."
"That is amazing," Adam said, "I really never knew.
Thank you for inventing it, goodbye." And off they flew.

The next inventor they went to see worked all through the night in his weird laboratory trying to make a light. "Hi Adam, I am Thomas Edison and you're just in time to see the invention of the light bulb using electricity."

He flicked a switch then Adam saw the light bulb flash and flicker.
"That's so cool! That so deserves a best invention sticker.
But we have some more inventors we have to go and meet
before our job to find the best inventor is complete."

They flew through time and space again and continued on their quest
and wondered which invention they thought could be the very best.
They landed on a dairy farm and met lazy milkmaid Maisy.
"Can someone help me please," she said, "to milk my moo cow Daisy."

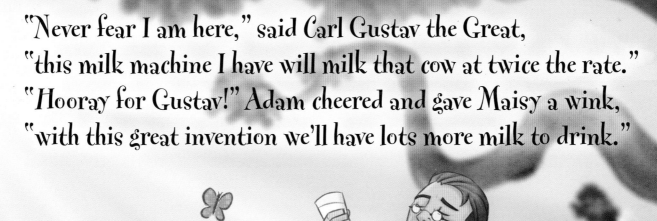

"Never fear I am here," said Carl Gustav the Great,
"this milk machine I have will milk that cow at twice the rate."
"Hooray for Gustav!" Adam cheered and gave Maisy a wink,
"with this great invention we'll have lots more milk to drink."

After lunch of yummy milk and a buttered jammy scone
the next invention they went to see was of the telephone.
"Quickly boys, come on in, this you have to see,
the invention of the best invention in all of history."

"Watson can you hear me? This is Alexander Bell."
"Yes," replied a funny voice, "I can hear you rather well."
"That's so cool! Your telephone will truly change the world,
well done," said Adam, "and goodbye." Then off they whizzed and whirled.

Spinning round and round and upside down back in time to history bound
when they landed on the ground they heard a rock 'n rolly sound.
Then Adam saw the great Steve Jobs with earphones in his ears.
"Adam," he said, "check these out, they're the best things out in years."

TOP SECRET

"We call them Apple iPods, iPads and iPhones
and when you use them fun and music run right through your bones."
"Holy Moly Guacamole!" with a giggle Adam said,
"these inventions could win 1st prize before I go to bed."

Then off they went once again flying through time and space,
when Adam saw the next invention you should have seen his face.
"Adam," said Louis Lumiere, "this invention is like no other,
which I invented with Auguste my famous bigger brother."

With a scream full of excitement Adam jumped with joy
"We're going to the movies oh boy! oh boy! oh boy!"
He took his seat and munched and crunched through popcorn treats galore
until his little tummy said, "I can't fit any more."

After filling up with popcorn treats they continued on their way
to the invention of the aeroplane on a cold December day.
"Look," said Adam, "over there, it's Orville and Wilbur Wright,
we're just in time to watch them make the world's 1st ever flight."

Adam held his breath and peaked out through one eye
as he really didn't think that Wilber's plane could ever fly.
It raced along the runway giving Adam such a scare
but, to everyone's amazement, it floated up into the air.

"Whoa ho!" Adam roared, "this plane must be the best,
I think it has to win 1st prize on our best invention quest.
Come on Fluff, take us home I think our job is done
but before we make our final call we better check with Mum."

With one last twirl and final swirl Fluff quickly flew them back
to their bedroom where they landed on their bottoms with a whack.
Mum and Dad raced up the stairs and said, "what is going on?
Adam, you should be fast asleep and how long have you been gone?"

"Mummy, Daddy," Adam said, "we travelled back through history
 and solved the best invention ever throughout history mystery."
"Oh sweet Adam," Mummy said in her very special way,
"The best invention is the hug or kiss we get each day.

But of all the great inventions, be them old or be them new,
the best invention ever is the love that gave me you."

Night, night, sleep tight, you make me smile
and make my whole world so worthwhile.
Sweet dreams, my love, I am truly blessed
Of all inventions you are the best.